There's Nothing to D~o~o~o!

WRITTEN BY Judith Mathews

ILLUSTRATED BY Kurt Cyrus

Browndeer Press
Harcourt Brace & Company
SAN DIEGO   NEW YORK   LONDON

To my calves,
Benjie, Anna, and Noah

—J. M.

Library of Congress Cataloging-in-Publication Data
Mathews, Judith.
There's nothing to *d-o-o-o!*/Judith Mathews; illustrated by Kurt Cyrus.
p.   cm.
"Browndeer Press."
Summary: Bored with seeing the same things all the time, a little calf sets off to find
something new, but discovers that she misses her mother and her familiar surroundings.
ISBN 0-15-201647-3
[1. Cows—Fiction.   2. Lost children—Fiction.]   I. Cyrus, Kurt, ill.   II. Title.
PZ7.M42517Th   1999
[E]—dc21   97-32540

First edition
A C E F D B
Printed in Singapore

The illustrations in this book were done in watercolor and
colored pencil on hot press 140 lb. watercolor paper.
The display type was set in Monotype Footlight Light.
The text type was set in Gill Sans.
Color separations by United Graphics Pte. Ltd., Singapore
Printed and bound by Tien Wah Press, Singapore
This book was printed on totally chlorine-free Nymolla Matte Art paper.
Production supervision by Stanley Redfern and Pascha Gerlinger
Designed by Lori McThomas Buley

Laloo lived on the farm with her mother, Mamoo. In the daytime, Laloo played with the lambs and calves in the pasture.

At night, she snuggled with Mamoo in the warm straw, and they sang this song together:

Chilly water from the pump,
Broken fences made to jump.

Mooing friends to mingle near,
And our woolly friends are here.

Corn as sweet as clover buds,
Juicy grass and chewy cuds.

Good night, barn and cows and sheep!
Now it's time to go to sleep.

Then Laloo and Mamoo closed their eyes.

One hot day, Laloo stood dozing under a tree. She swatted flies with her tail and stared at a spot on the ground. When she looked up, she saw the same old calves, the same old pasture, the same old barn.

"There's nothing to *d-o-o-o*!" she moaned to her mama.

Mamoo gazed at her daughter. "Chew your cud," said Mamoo. "Count your stomachs as the green grass travels through you. Have a daydream under the tree. That's what cows *d-o-o-o*."

that didn't satisfy Laloo. "I want
something *n-e-w*," she said. She slipped
through the broken place in the fence
and ran away.

Laloo trotted down the road until she came to a wild field. A young mouse scurried by.

"Is this your field?" asked Laloo.

"No," said the mouse. "But this is where I live, and it's the best field anywhere. See for yourself."

Laloo raced into the high weeds. She
mowed a twisted trail. She smelled a million
new flowers, and she munched on sweet grass.

Soon Laloo got hot and thirsty. She thought of Mamoo and the water trough next to the barn. "But I want something *n-e-w*," said Laloo to herself.

There was a shady forest right nearby, and Laloo could hear the song of a stream inside. She followed the tune.

A raccoon sat by the water, washing his hands.
"Is this your stream?" asked Laloo.
"No," said the raccoon. "But I live nearby, and
it's the best stream anywhere. See for yourself."

Laloo drank and drank. She made big splashes in the shallow water. She followed fish that darted downstream.

After a while, though, she got sleepy. Laloo walked along until she came to a ravine. It was cool and quiet at the bottom.

She thought of Mamoo and their warm straw bed back home. "But I want something *n-e-w*," she whispered to the fallen leaves.

Laloo skittered down the slope and fell
asleep, hidden by shadows.

Back on the farm, Mamoo saw the sun dip toward the barn. "La-*looo*, where are *y-o-o-o*?" she called. But Laloo was too far away to hear.

Mamoo stepped over the broken place
in the fence and walked along the road.

At the wild field, she spotted Laloo's trail. Mamoo stepped into the high weeds and called, "La-*looo,* where are *y-o-o-o?*" But Laloo was too far away to hear.

At the forest's edge, Mamoo listened to the
stream and followed it deeper into the forest.
"La-*looo*, where are *y-o-o-o*?" she called. But
Laloo was too far away to hear.

Mamoo walked on through the forest. She came to the ravine full of dark and dappled leaves. Mamoo slid down the side. And there she found Laloo.

Mamoo sang softly into Laloo's ear:

Chilly water from the pump,
Broken fences made to jump.

Calves and lambs are waiting near,
Hoping you will soon appear.

Corn as sweet as clover buds,
Juicy grass and chewy cuds.

See the world someday! But now
It's home sweet barn, my little cow.

And Laloo opened her eyes.

"Mamoo!" she said. "I missed our straw bed and our water trough. And I missed *y-o-o-o*."

Mamoo nuzzled Laloo, and Laloo nuzzled back.

"I think I'll go home now," Laloo said, "and see the rest another day."

"Another day," said Mamoo.

"*S-o-o-o-n*," said Laloo.

"Very *s-o-o-o-n*," said Mamoo.

And they started home.